This book belongs to

_____

DISNEY PRESENTS A **PIXAR** FILM

A READ-ALOUD STORYBOOK

Adapted by Lisa Marsoli
Illustrated by the Disney Storybook Artists
Designed by Tony Fejeran of Disney Publishing's Global Design Group
Inspired by the art and character designs created by Pixar Animation Studios

Random House 🏠 New York

Library of Congress Control Number: 2005937885   ISBN: 0-7364-2338-9   ISBN-13: 978-0-7364-2338-0

www.randomhouse.com/kids/disney

Printed in the United States of America

10 9 8 7 6 5 4 3 2 1

The biggest car race of the year—the Dinoco 400—was about to begin. Cars of all makes and models packed the stadium, ready to cheer on their favorite racers.

Rookie Lightning McQueen was in his trailer revving up. "I am speed," the race car repeated to himself. "I am Lightning."

Finally, he burst into the stadium. Camera flashes went off all around. The crowd went wild!

Meanwhile, The King, who had been the number one champion race car for years, was at the Dinoco stage, surrounded by reporters. His sponsor, Dinoco, had made him famous, but it was time to move on. He was ready to retire, and this would be his last race.

Chick Hicks was thrilled that The King was retiring. Chick was famous for two things: always coming in second and always playing dirty. Having lived in The King's shadow for years, the ruthless race car was ready to make his move. Chick was focused on getting the Piston Cup and beating out McQueen for the legendary Dinoco sponsorship, as well as the fame and fortune that came with them.

VA-RRoom! Soon the cars were off and racing. McQueen raced ahead and burst past Chick. Angrily, Chick bumped McQueen off the track. Moving quickly, the rookie got back into the race—only to face a massive pileup . . . purposely caused by Chick.

"Get through *that*, McQueen," Chick muttered as he headed in for a pit stop. Amazingly, McQueen weaved his way through the wrecked cars—and took the lead!

But while the remaining race cars went to the pits, McQueen kept going.

McQueen finally drove in for a pit stop.

"No tires! Just the gas!" he shouted to his crew.

It was a risky move. Too risky. During the last lap, McQueen's two rear tires blew out! The King and Chick quickly closed in on him. McQueen even stuck out his tongue to gain an edge.

"It's too close to call!" cried the announcer.

While the instant replay was analyzed, McQueen boasted to the reporters, "I'm a one-man show."

Furious, his pit crew quit right then and there.

"You ain't gonna win unless you got good folks behind you," The King said to the rookie. "Let them do their job." But McQueen wasn't listening. He was busy dreaming of victory . . .

. . . until the announcer reported that it was a three-way tie! McQueen groaned. He, The King, and Chick would all go to California for a tiebreaker race.

McQueen couldn't wait to win the race and earn the snazzy Dinoco sponsorship.

But for now, he had another sponsor. He rolled into the Rust-eze tent and flashed a forced smile: "Use Rust-eze and you too can look like me!"

Many long hours later, McQueen's driver, Mack, was driving the rookie along the highway to California. Mack wanted to stop for some sleep, but McQueen refused.

"We're driving all night," McQueen insisted.

So the big truck pushed forward. As he fought to keep his eyes open, a gang of cars lulled him to sleep and then began bumping into him. Suddenly, one of the pranksters sneezed. Startled awake, Mack swerved dangerously . . .

. . . and McQueen, asleep in the back, rolled out onto the Interstate! The race car awoke to the sight of traffic barreling toward him. Terrified, he looked for Mack. He thought he saw him going down an exit ramp and quickly followed. But it wasn't Mack!

Lost, McQueen ended up on the old Highway 66.

That was when he noticed flashing lights behind him.

BANG! BANG! BANG! The Sheriff's tailpipe backfired.

"Why is he shooting at me?" McQueen panicked and zoomed recklessly down the main street of a little town, dragging a statue of the town's founder behind him, destroying the road. He stopped only when he got caught between two telephone poles.

"Boy, you're in a heap of trouble," said the Sheriff.

The next morning, McQueen woke up locked inside the town's impound lot.

"My name's Mater," a friendly tow truck said.

"Where am I?" McQueen grimaced at the rusty truck.

"Radiator Springs," Mater replied proudly. Just then, the Sheriff arrived. It was time for McQueen to go to court.

The courthouse was filled with angry townsfolk. They were upset that McQueen had ruined the road. When the judge, Doc Hudson, saw that McQueen was a race car, he quickly ordered him to leave . . . but then Sally, the town attorney, arrived.

JUSTITAE VIA STRATA VERIT

"Make this guy fix the road," the blue sports car said. Sally told everyone that their little forgotten town needed business. Without a road, there would be no travelers, which meant no business.

Doc made his ruling: McQueen couldn't leave Radiator Springs until he fixed the road.

McQueen soon met Bessie—the massive road-paving machine he would have to haul to smooth out the road.

It was no wonder that when Mater took off McQueen's parking boot, the race car drove away as fast as he could . . . until he ran out of fuel. The Sheriff had taken the gas out of McQueen while he was asleep.

With no way to escape, McQueen began to work.

When a minivan couple drove into town, the cars of Radiator Springs shifted into high gear.

"Customers!" shouted Sally. The cars desperately tried to sell the visitors fuel, tires, new paint jobs—but the couple just wanted directions to the Interstate.

Later that day, McQueen heard a radio report that Chick was already in California, practicing for the race. So the race car pulled Bessie extra hard for one hour, then announced that he was done. But the road *wasn't* done. It was a mess.

"It looks awful!" exclaimed Sally.

"Now it looks like the rest of the town," McQueen replied rudely.

Insulted, Doc stared long and hard at McQueen. Then he challenged the young hotshot to a race. "If you win, you go and I fix the road. If I win, you do the road *my* way," he said.

Out at the dirt track, McQueen took a quick lead. But when he made a sharp turn, he skidded into a ditch.

"You drive like you fix roads," said Doc, looking down at the rookie. "Lousy."

Humiliated, McQueen went back to work. He scraped up the mess he'd made and started to pave the road once again. The next morning, the townsfolk awoke to a smooth, newly paved section of road. Even Doc was impressed. But where was McQueen?

He was out practicing the turn he'd missed when he had raced Doc. Watching McQueen miss the turn again, Doc offered some advice: "Turn right to go left." Reluctantly, McQueen tried it—and wiped out! Giving up, he returned to paving the road. And as he did, the townsfolk began to spruce up their shops. They were taking new pride in their town.

Suddenly, Red the fire engine sprayed icy cold water on the filthy, cactus-prickled McQueen.

"If you want to stay at the Cozy Cone, you gotta be clean," Sally said. She owned the motel and thought that McQueen might want to stay there instead of at the impound. She was starting to like him and the effect he was having on the town.

"You're being nice to me!" a surprised McQueen said.

That night, Mater took McQueen tractor tipping for fun.
Then the truck showed off his backward driving.

"Maybe I'll use it in my big race," McQueen said about
Mater's driving technique. "I'll be the first rookie in history
ever to win it. We're talking a big new sponsor with private
helicopters. . . ."

McQueen even promised Mater a helicopter ride.

"I knowed I made a good choice," Mater told McQueen.

"In what?" asked McQueen.

"My best friend," said Mater. McQueen smiled as Mater
drove away. A best friend!

When McQueen finally drove to Sally's motel, he discovered that she had overheard the conversation.

"Did you mean it? That you'll get him a ride?" she asked, confronting him.

"Oh, who knows?" McQueen said casually.

"Mater trusts you." Sally turned to leave.

"Thanks for letting me stay here!" McQueen said quickly.

"Good night," Sally replied.

The next morning, while McQueen was waiting for his daily gas ration, he wandered into Doc's back garage. And then he saw it: a grimy old Piston Cup. The plaque read, The Hudson Hornet, Champion: 1951. There were Piston Cups from 1952 and 1953, too. McQueen couldn't believe it. Doc was a famous race car champion!

When Doc found McQueen, he was furious. "The sign says, stay out!"

"You're the Hudson Hornet! You still hold the record for most wins in a single season!" McQueen babbled.

"All I see is a bunch of empty cups," Doc grumbled as he pushed McQueen outside and slammed the garage door.

Bursting with excitement, McQueen told everyone in town who Doc was. But they all thought he was crazy.

That was when Sally arrived and gave McQueen a full tank of gas. McQueen could have sped out of town . . . but he didn't. Instead, he happily followed Sally through the mountains, finally enjoying the beauty of his surroundings.

"The Wheel Well Motel," Sally said, showing McQueen a broken-down building. "It used to be the most popular stop on the Mother Road."

Then Sally told McQueen that she had been a big-shot attorney in Los Angeles. On a drive across the country, she'd landed in Radiator Springs. It was the first time she had truly felt like she was home.

Sally explained that the big Interstate outside of town hadn't always existed. Before, Highway 66 had been the main road, and in its heyday, it had been something special. "Back then cars didn't drive on it to make great time. They drove on it to have a great time. Then the town got bypassed just to save ten minutes of driving." Sally sighed. "One of these days we'll find a way to get back on the map."

Later that afternoon, McQueen spotted Doc wearing racing tires at the dirt track. Ducking out of sight, the rookie watched Doc maneuver effortlessly around the tricky curve that had given McQueen so much trouble.

"Wow! You're amazing!" exclaimed McQueen.

Doc turned without a word and raced off.

McQueen followed Doc back to his office. "How could a car like you quit at the top of your game?" he asked.

"You think I quit? They quit on *me*," Doc replied bitterly. McQueen listened as Doc told him about his big wreck. When Doc had recovered, the racing world had told him that he had been replaced by a rookie—a rookie like McQueen.

The next morning, a beautiful, newly paved main road stretched from one end of Radiator Springs to the other.

"Good riddance," muttered Doc, happy that the race car appeared to have finished the job and left town.

But McQueen hadn't left. He became the best customer Radiator Springs had seen in a long time.

He got new tires, some of Fillmore's organic fuel, supplies at Sarge's, bumper stickers at Lizzie's, and a paint job at Ramone's.

"What do you think?" McQueen asked, surprising Sally with his makeover. "Radiator Springs looks pretty good on me."

"It looks like you've helped everybody in town," Sally said gratefully.

On McQueen's cue, the shopkeepers turned on their newly fixed neon signs—just as they had done in Radiator Springs' heyday. It was time to cruise! Everyone slowly and happily drove up and down the street.

It all seemed close to perfect . . . .

. . . until a wall of headlights approached the town.

"We have found McQueen!" boomed a voice from a helicopter. Crowds of reporters swarmed the small town.

"I'm sorry I lost you, boss," a relieved Mack said as soon as he reached the rookie. And on Mack's speakerphone, McQueen's agent, Harv, told him to get to the race fast: "Get out of Radiator Stinks now, or Dinoco's history!"

Fighting his way through the reporters, McQueen found Sally. But he didn't know what to say.

"I hope you find what you're looking for," Sally told him. She turned and disappeared into the crowd.

"Sally!" McQueen called after her, but it was too late. Sally was gone, and the reporters were closing in on him.

As Mack pulled out of town with McQueen, the reporters followed—except one, who stopped to thank Doc for calling her. Sally was stunned.

"You did this?" she asked.

"It's best for everyone," replied Doc.

"Best for everyone? Or best for you?" challenged Sally.

Radiator Springs was quiet once more.

"I didn't get to say goodbye to him," Mater said sadly.

Everyone but Doc went home silently and turned off the lights. The hope and happiness that had filled the air that night were gone. Doc felt ashamed as he realized how much McQueen had done for their town.

Soon McQueen was at the Los Angeles International Speedway, in the middle of the biggest race of his life. But his heart wasn't in it. The King and Chick were taking over the track. McQueen couldn't stop thinking about Sally and the friends he had left behind.

Suddenly, he found himself headed straight for a wall!

As he recovered, McQueen heard a familiar voice over his radio. It was Doc! All of McQueen's Radiator Springs friends had come to be his crew! And when the fans saw that Doc—the Fabulous Hudson Hornet—was the crew chief, they gave a roaring cheer.

Doc focused on McQueen. "If you can drive as good as you can fix a road, then you can win this race with your eyes shut!" he shouted.

51 FABULOUS HUDSON HORNET

McQueen took off with new determination. When Chick bumped him off the track, he used the "turn *right* to go *left*" trick. He even drove backward like Mater.

But just as he was about to cross the finish line and win, he stopped. Chick had caused The King to crash. As Chick zoomed ahead, McQueen sped back toward The King and pushed him across the finish line.

Chick finally won his Piston Cup, but the fans booed him! McQueen joined his friends at the Rust-eze tent. He had never felt happier. And when Tex, the owner of Dinoco, asked, "How'd you like to become the new face of Dinoco?" McQueen graciously said no. He decided to stay loyal to the Rust-eze gang, who had believed in him from the beginning . . . though he did ask Tex for one small favor.

Back at the Wheel Well, Sally was looking out over the valley when she heard a voice say, "I hear this place is back on the map." It was McQueen! "There's a rumor floating around that some hotshot Piston Cup race car is setting up his big racing headquarters here."

The two cars smiled happily at each other.

That was when Mater came flying by—in a Dinoco helicopter!

"He's my best friend," McQueen said, laughing. Sally smiled. The cocky race car had finally learned about friendship . . . and he'd learned that life was not just about being fast, but also about slowing down to enjoy things.

McQueen was home at last.